Being A Teen Isn't EASY

By April Debrow

Illustrated By KD

Copyright @ 2019 by April Debrow

Printed in USA aprilatvoice@gmail.com

Table of Contents

Introduction

Life can be difficult as a teen. Growing up, I didn't have anybody to talk to or confide in. Yes, I had friends but, as a teen you try to keep things in because, basically you don't know who to trust. Besides, girls love to gossip.

I decided to get some honest feedback from real teens about life as they viewed it. And, I wasn't quite ready for their answer's. I sat down with three different teen girls, all from different racial backgrounds, to compare the struggles that teens face today.

Girls feel an overwhelming pressure to be smart, beautiful, popular and mature. That pressure, from parents, peers, and social media, can lead to depression, eating disorders, self-mutilation and sexual experiences that happen too soon.

"I wrote this book in hope that other teen-agers would see themselves in these brave young ladies and parents can see beyond their daughter's rebellion stage.

Life is hard being a teen-ager especially with social media being so popular.

I want you to listen to each story that is being shared by each teen and at the end think about somebody each girl may remind you of. I pray that you decide to pass this along to a teen who needs to hear from other peers who they share the same trials with.

Julie

Meet Julie-Julie is a 15-year-old bi-racial female who lives in a two-parent home but, she still struggles with finding herself. Both parents work long hours daily and sometimes on the weekend.

Julie is missing out on time with them and wish that they would just take time out of their busy schedule and take her places. Julie struggles with self-esteem issues and body image.

Life has been hard for her since she could remember. Julie explains, that the kids at school make it hard for her to participate in PE due to her weight issues.

Julie explained that she prays every day before she walks into her classes, with hopes of just one day without being judged.

She never wanted to attend that school, it was her parents who decided that it was best for her in the long run, to attend an all-girls catholic school.

Julie wants to attend her old public school but, since her parents are all about their image, she must continue to pretend she's happy. It's exhausting says Julie. "I am dying inside; nobody listens or cares about my feelings"!

As you see things aren't as it appears sometimes. Julie cannot be a teen and she truly hasn't had the opportunity to be able express the feelings that she's held in for years.

What parents fail to realize, is that we must be active in our children's lives. Julie is a

prime example of a child who will one day resent her parents for not being there for her. She went on to explaining her daily schedule.

Julie wakes up at five thirty every morning, get dressed, brush her teeth, fix her own breakfast and lunch for the day, wait outside for her moms' friend to pick her up, then proceeds to be the victim to bulling. Then repeat it all over again.

Once the weekend arrives, Julie either plays with her dog or read a book or two. No outside play or hangouts with friends like normal teens.

Visually I can see the toll that teen life is having on Julie and I can't help but feel the need to say something to her parents but, who am I to stir-up trouble?

Julie closed by saying, "thank you for letting me speak"!

"Greatness is not for the chosen few but for the few who choose it." To me greatness just means being successful in your goals while staying true to wholesome values.

You don't have to be famous, popular or even rich to be great. You just have to live with integrity and do your best in what you do. That's greatness.

Voice

Use it to tell your story!

This image should never be of your daughter, granddaughter,

niece, sister, cousin, best friend or classmate.

We are powerful and our VOICES are loud!

Nicole

As I began to prepare to speak to Nicole, the situation became clear to me that she was nervous and contemplating not saying a word.

But, quickly said "okay let's get this over with". Nicole is a 16-year-old Latina girl with two younger twin brothers. She's very outgoing and hates boys!

I asked her why, didn't she care for boys and she replied, "I just don't".

Nicole-Nicki for short began to explain that she lives with her mom and her twin brothers live her dad.

Her parents divorced when Nicole was twelve years old and she hated that she had to stay with her mom! Her dad was her best friend and she felt that her mom ran him off with her constant nagging. Nichole was adamant that her life is horrible and how she can't wait until she turns eighteen.

Once she turns eighteen, she will move far away from her mom. Nicole's body language was that of an angry, sad unheard teen.

As our conversation continued, I asked Nichole how often does she see her dad? And, she replied "once every month". Then Nichole went on to saying, "It's due to my mom being a bitch"!

I could tell that Nichole wasn't too fond of her mother and I tried my best to change the subject by asking her about her grades and how she liked school?

But that didn't work. Nicole wanted to release all the resentment that she felt towards her mom that day.

I sat there for an hour just allowing her to get it out. Once she finished, our conversation shifted back to her hate for boys.

Nicole began to tear up and I asked her, "if she wanted me to finish up another day? Of course, she said no so, I proceeded by letting her finish.

Nicole went into detail about how she was taken advantage of by her moms' current boyfriends' adult brother. She explained being in her room, when he came in and locked the door behind him. She yelled at him to get out but, no one heard her because, her mom was at work and her stepdad went to the gym. After she realized that he was probably going to attempt to hurt her. She reached for her phone. But he slapped it out of her hand and proceeded to throw her on the bed ripping off her shirt.

Once he was successful with exposing her, he began to pull at her underwear. Nicole stated, "I was numb through it all".

When he was finished, he laid on top of me with his hand around my throat, threatening to kill me and my mom if I told.

But I didn't care what he said, I told my counselor at my school the next day and she called my mom to the school.

When my mom arrived, my counselor told her what happened and my mom said, "she's a liar"! I was crushed and angry! How could she say that I thought? So, since then I just hated her more! I asked my counselor if she could call my dad?

Once my dad came, I was able to leave with him but, that didn't last long. His new wife and I didn't get along at all and, I ended up back with my mom after she split-up with her boyfriend and she put his brother out.

It was rocky for the first two months. But I had no choice but, to stay with her. So, I sucked up my feelings and stayed in my room.

It's been five months and I still hate her, and I can't wait until I turn eighteen. Everything is hard, living with her and, going to school dealing with stupid classmates, and the teachers totally make me sick!

Nicole was able to speak up about things that caused her shame and misfortunes in her early years of being a teen. Being a teen is hard and, the added trauma doesn't make it any easier.

Ivory

Meet Ivory, she's a 17-year-old black queen. Ivory was ready and excited to talk about her life as a teen! Ivory began by saying "I am a black queen who loves life"! I live with my grandma and my three brothers. My grandma got custody of us when my mom went to prison. My dad got shot when I was three years old, they say he robbed a store but, I've heard so many stories that I don't know what to believe.

Ivory went on to saying that she wants to go to college to pursue her nursing degree. She currently works at McDonalds part time because, her grandmothers on a fixed income, which makes it hard for her to buy the things that they need.

She hasn't seen her mom in six years, and she misses her a lot. Ivory is a good student who adores her seventh period teacher Ms. Roe. Ms. Roe helps her stay focused in school and, she takes up time with Ivory after school as well.

"I didn't like myself and I had a thousand reasons, "she said. I was just not turning out to be the person I wanted to be. "Eventually, the depression lifted after I decided to focus on what I wanted for my future.

Ivory recently received her learners permit and, she's super excited and can't wait to save enough money to purchase a car. In the meanwhile, Ivory is anticipating her senior year to be smooth because, she's ahead on her credits and she earned the ability to get out of school early.

She went on to explaining her love for her brothers and the need to become a successful individual. Thank you, Ivory, for sharing!

Believe
in yourself
&
you will be
Unstoppable

Life is different from person to person. I had the pleasure of speaking to three different young ladies, who live totally different lives but, have so much in common.

We look at everyone around us and think we live a life with no similarities when in fact, we're all similar in some way. Yes, our skin color is different but, our lives are full of doubt, disappointment, uncertainty, love, hate and the list goes on. If you find yourself unable to express your feelings to another human being, write it down and watch the instant relief you receive; just by getting it out.

There's also more pressure that follows into adulthood. Which includes, what to do after you finish school, what job to pursue, what college to attend, what if I fail. Are all struggles of teen/pre-adult hood.

The feminist movement came with some incredible benefits, but it has downfalls as well. I personally think there's more pressure to be a mini adult from the time we're very young." And, it doesn't help much when you're subjected to un-fortunate situations along the way.

After listening to each teen girl in some discussion groups that I had the pleasure of attending. One girl stood out for me. She had the courage to confront a male teacher for his sexist behavior and several filed a complaint with the principal about boys who were repeatedly harassing them in the halls. Which is good sign that girls are finally able to use their voice to speak up.

It gives me joy to hear how aware and responsible these girls are. The Me-Too Movement has certainly opened a lot of doors for such accomplishments around the world. But there's always something else lurking in the background and that's the need to fit in. Body image is a big craze!

Thin is in so the world says. Which brings on more mental agony to girls in general. Teen-age girls don't stand a chance in this world. They go from getting pass one thing and fail into being subjected to anorexia and bulimia which has increased in the last 15 years, probably due to a greater recognition that bulimia is a disease that must be treated.

But I've noticed lately that there is more plus size models and actresses so, that's a great start to the "you must look a certain way epidemic.

It is hard to prove, scientifically, that it's more stressful to be a teen-ager now than it ever was. Being a teen-age girl is impossible to put into one sentence, "That's why I decided to do a one on one with teen girls and attend groups with-in my area. This is a never-ending topic and I truly believe girls rock!

Resources Social Media pages:

The Atlas of Beauty

Amy Poehler's Smart Girls

A Mighty Girl

Team Girls

Websites for teens:

Helpguide.org

LoveisRespect.com

Safeteens.com

Teensaginstbulling.com

Teenhelp.com

Date: _____

_____
_____
_____
_____
_____
_____
_____
_____
_____
_____
_____
_____
_____

_____
_____
_____
_____
_____
_____
_____
_____
_____
_____
_____
_____

Date: _____

Date: _____

_____

_____

_____

_____

_____

_____

_____

_____

_____

_____

_____

_____

_____

_____

_____

_____

_____

_____

_____

_____

_____

_____

_____

Date: _____

_____

_____

_____

_____

_____

_____

_____

_____

_____

_____

_____

_____

_____

_____

_____

_____

_____

_____

_____

_____

_____

Date: _____

Date: _____

_____
_____
_____
_____
_____
_____
_____
_____
_____
_____
_____
_____
_____

_____
_____
_____
_____
_____
_____
_____
_____
_____
_____

CHOOSE A QUIET PLACE
ALLOW 10 MIN. FREE OF DISTRACTION
SIT OR LIE DOWN COMFORTABLY
HAVE GOOD POSTURE
CLOSE YOUR EYES
BREATH IN THROUGH NOSE
FILLING LUNGS WITH NEW AIR
EXHALE THROUGH MOUTH
FOCUS ON YOUR BREATH
BREATH IN
AND BREATH OUT
ALLOW YOUR THOUGHTS TO FADE
SLOWLY OPEN YOUR EYES WHEN YOU ARE
FINISHED

A special gift for you

To

From

A GOOD TEACHER

Is one whose ears get as

Much exercise as her mouth."

USE YOUR VOICE TO TELL YOUR STORY!

Thank you

Thank you to Ivory, Nicole and Julie for sharing your life with everyone. I know that it is difficult to be a teen. But, you guys do it well despite your circumstances. To all teen-aged girls around the world, keep your head up and be the best you!

Life is about choices and I want all girls to (MGC) make good choices. And, remember to write in your journals daily.

I want to acknowledge all survivors of molestation/rape. You guys inspire me each day to continue to use my voice and advocate for the voiceless.

To my boys and my husband, thank you for putting up with my long hours on the computer. But most importantly, thank you GOD for wisdom and forgiveness!

April Debrow is an Author, advocate, survivor, wife, and mother. April is a native of Arcadia, Fl. And, she currently resides in Daytona Beach, Fl. April holds an Associate degree, & Certifications as a Human Service Addiction Specialist, Human Traffic Awareness Advocate, Mental Health First aide, Domestic Violence Advocate, and she's currently pursuing her BSW. April is adamant about prevention & protecting for all victims of abuse. April's motto is "Use your voice to tell your story!

53389302R00021